Do

the Cake

Written by Jill Eggleton
Illustrated by Raymond McGrath

Rigby

It was Dad's birthday.
"I have twenty friends
coming to my party,"
said Dad.
"I'll have to make
a **big** cake."

“I know,” said Dad.
“I’ll make it like a castle.”

“We’ll help,” said the kids.

So Dad and the kids made
a cake like a castle.
The cake was so big,
they had to make
a bucket of icing.

"It looks good," said Dad.
"My friends will like it."
He put the cake
in the pantry.

But the next day, when Dad
went to the pantry,
there were ants everywhere.
They were all over the cake.
Some were running up and
down and some were stuck
in the icing.

"I'll get the vacuum cleaner," said Dad.

"**No! No! No!**" said the kids. "Not again!"

Dad took the cake outside.
"I know," said Dad.
"I'll get the hair dryer.
It will blow the ants off."

Dad put the hair dryer on the cake.
"**Stop!**" shouted the kids.
"There are still ants everywhere, and look at the icing!"

Dad went to the shed.
"I know," he said.
"I'll get the big blower.
This will get them off."

Dad put the blower
on the cake, but
whooooosh ...
the ants **and** the cake
went up in the air!

There was cake on the gate,
cake on the trees, and
cake on the roof!

When Dad's friends came,
there were birds everywhere.

"Dad blew up his cake,"
said the kids.
"And the birds
are having the party!"

Dad's friends laughed.
"We don't have presents
for you," they said.
"But we did make you
a big cake."

"Let's eat it **now!**"
said the kids.

A Comic Strip

Guide Notes

Title: Dad and the Cake
Stage: Early (4) – Green

Genre: Fiction
Approach: Guided Reading
Processes: Thinking Critically, Exploring Language, Processing Information
Written and Visual Focus: Comic Strip

THINKING CRITICALLY

(sample questions)

- What do you think this story could be about? Look at the title and discuss.
- Look at the cover. How do you know Dad and the kids are happy with the cake?
- Look at pages 2 and 3. Why do you think Dad wants to make the cake like a castle?
- Look at pages 4 and 5. Why do you think Dad says his friends will like the cake?
- Look at pages 6 and 7. Why do you think the kids told Dad not to use the vacuum cleaner?
- Look at pages 8 and 9. Why do you think the kids said to "look at the icing"?
- Look at pages 10 and 11. What else do you think Dad could have used to get the ants off the cake?
- Look at page 14. Why do you think the kids said that they should eat the cake now?

EXPLORING LANGUAGE

Terminology

Title, cover, illustrations, author, illustrator

Vocabulary

Interest words: castle, icing, pantry, vacuum cleaner, dryer, blower
High-frequency words: friend, everywhere, know
Positional words: over, up, down, off, on, in
Compound words: birthday, everywhere, outside

Print Conventions

Capital letter for sentence beginnings and names (**D**ad), periods, commas, exclamation marks, quotation marks, ellipsis, possessive apostrophes